Mighty Jack

climbs
Mount Everest

Written by: Jason Timmerman | Illustrated and designed by: Rachel Nehl

Story Copyright © 2014 Jason Timmerman | Illustration and design Copyright © 2014 Rachel Nehl

ISBN-13: 978-1500122836
ISBN-10: 15001222831

Jack,

May your life always be filled
with amazing adventures.

– J.T.

It was a cold and sunny June day on Mount Everest, the highest mountain in the world.

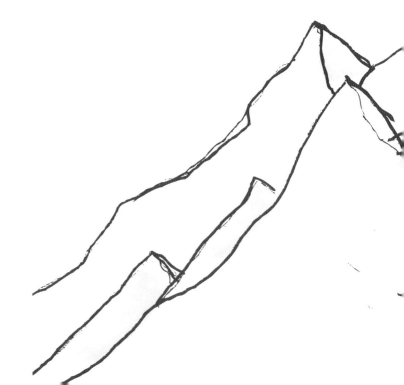

Mighty Jack and his crew awoke and crawled out of their tents. They were excited about the big day ahead.

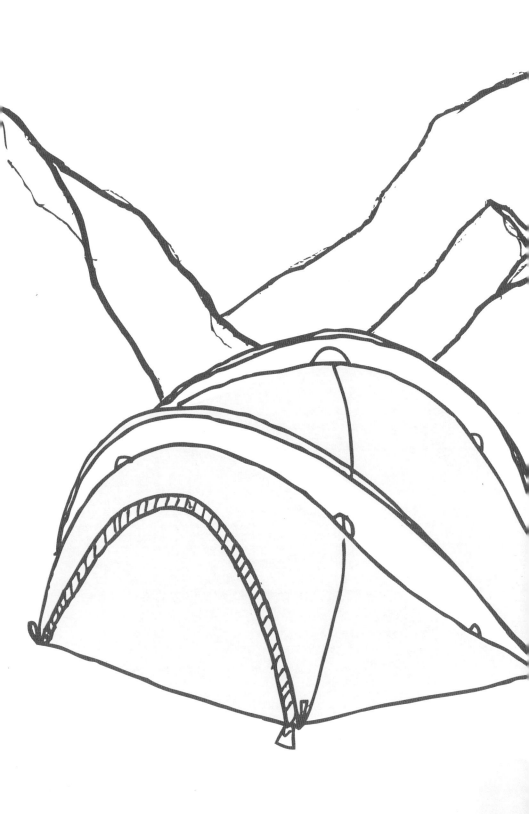

They put on their special glasses
to protect their eyes from the sun
reflecting off the snow.

Ethan and Owen checked the weather
report. A big storm was on the way.
Today was their last chance to make
a push for the summit.

Jack said, "OK boys, are you ready?"

Ethan replied, "You bet!"

Owen said, "Let's go!"

The three brave adventurers
started up the mountain.

Soon they reached a crevasse. One at a time, they carefully walked on a wobbly ladder across the deep hole.

Jack stumbled into the crevasse!

Luckily, a Sherpa was there
to help him get out.

Safely across, the boys exchanged
high fives. Owen said, "**Great job
guys — that was a close one.**"

The wind picked up as the boys
climbed up the next set of ropes.
They were slowly getting closer
to the top.

The air was getting very thin now, and it was time to put on their oxygen masks and helmets.

They were now in the most dangerous part of the climb — the **Death Zone**. The boys paused to take a break and prepare for the challenge ahead.

Ethan said, "We're almost there — we can do it!" Jack replied, "I'm ready to rock and roll — let's finish it off!"

Slowly, the boys marched their way to the top.

After what seemed like forever,
they reached the summit! Jack
yelled, "Woohoo, we made it!"
Ethan exclaimed, "Oh yeah,
baby!" Owen shouted, "We're
the youngest to reach the top!"

The boys high-fived each other and
celebrated loudly. But then they
heard a loud rumbling noise that
silenced their cheers. **Was it an ...**

It was no avalanche —
it was Jack's parents
running into the
living room!
They exclaimed,
"Hey, what's all the
ruckus? What are
you boys doing?"

"But, Mom! We're just climbing Mount Everest,"
Jack replied quietly. Looking at the boys' long
faces, Jack's mom said, "OK, that's fine."

"Just make sure to clean up this mess when you're done." "Sure thing, Mom! We will," Jack replied happily.

With their quest complete,
the boys headed down the
mountain and celebrated with
some cookies and hot chocolate.

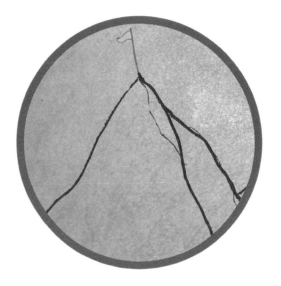

The author would like to acknowledge
all of the real-life Everest climbers.
Your courage and sense of adventure
were an inspiration for this book.

Made in the USA
Lexington, KY
20 June 2015